The Tennessee Tornado
Wilma Rudolph

by Jo Pitkin

 HOUGHTON MIFFLIN   BOSTON

DON'T BLINK!

The year 1960 was like a dream for Wilma Rudolph. Just twenty years old, she was the star of the United States Olympic track team. Rudolph was already a veteran Olympic sprinter. She had competed in the 1956 games in Melbourne, Australia and had come away with a bronze medal. Now, late in the summer of 1960, she and her teammates flew to Rome, Italy, eager for the games to begin.

From the start of the Olympics, Wilma captivated the crowds. Fans loved her easy-going charm, her warm smile, and her dignity. When she appeared on the field for her races, the huge audience roared. In the deafening noise, they chanted her name over and over. Television viewers and sports fans were warned: Don't blink! You might miss her.

Wilma Rudolph sprints from the starting blocks during a qualifying heat at the 1960 Summer Olympics in Rome.

When she did run, Wilma burned up the track. She was unstoppable in her specialties, the sprints and the relays. She won all her races, taking three gold medals. No woman would win three golds in the same Olympics again for nearly thirty years. By the end of the 1960 Olympics, Wilma Rudolph was known as the fastest woman in the world.

Basking in the golden Roman sunlight, Rudolph seemed like a natural. She was bright, a gifted athlete who possessed both poise and beauty. These were the first Olympics to be televised worldwide, and Rudolph's charm was perfect for the new medium. She instantly gained fans around the globe. To them, Wilma Rudolph made it all look easy.

Getting to the Olympics had been far from easy, however. Wilma was blessed with great talent, but her success was the result of hard work. And her charm and grace hid her fierce determination. "*I can't* are two words that have never been in my personality," she once said. In fourth grade, Wilma had a teacher known as Mrs. Hoskins, the "meanest, toughest teacher in the whole school." Though she was feared by the other students, she earned Wilma's affection because she was the only teacher who didn't play favorites—she treated every-one equally. Mrs. Hoskins always told Wilma, "Do it. Don't daydream about it." That positive thinking stuck with Wilma, and carried her through life.

FIGHTING POLIO

Wilma Glodean Rudolph needed every ounce of that determination. She was born into a large family on June 23, 1940, in Tennessee. At birth she weighed only four-and-a-half pounds. As a child, it seemed that Wilma was always sick. She had colds, mumps, measles, and scarlet fever. To her brothers and sisters—Wilma had twenty-one of them—she was the sickly one.

Wilma battled each illness. Then polio struck her when she was just four. Polio is a disease that attacks the central nervous system, damaging the nerve cells of the brain and spinal cord. It can cause muscle weakness and paralysis. In Wilma's time, there was no cure for polio. The disease left many young people disabled for life.

Polio left Wilma's left leg twisted. She had to wear a heavy steel brace to straighten her leg. Doctors told Wilma's parents that their daughter would never walk without it.

Wilma wanted to prove the doctors wrong. She wanted to walk like other children more than anything. To help her leg heal and grow stronger, Wilma endured years of painful therapy.

Every week, Wilma and her mother rode a bus to a hospital in Nashville. There Wilma received heat and whirlpool treatments. "They were forever pulling, turning, twisting, lifting that leg," Wilma remembered. At home, Wilma's family took turns massaging her leg four times a day.

Wilma Rudolph at age 21, five years after her first Olympics.

The hospital in Nashville was the nearest one that treated African Americans. But it was still fifty miles from Wilma's home. During the long bus rides, Wilma learned about segregation firsthand. The bus station had separate ticket windows and waiting areas for whites and blacks. Wilma and her mother were forced to sit at the back of the bus.

After four years of treatment, Wilma's leg was much stronger. At age twelve, she removed her leg brace for good. Her mother wrapped the brace carefully in a box and sent it back to the hospital. "I was free at last," said Wilma.

BECOMING AN ATHLETE

Entering seventh grade at Burt High School, Wilma felt like a new person. She no longer wore a leg brace. She walked and ran like other children. And she fell in love with sports.

At first, her favorite sport was basketball. Wilma first learned how to play by watching the other kids on the playground. While she watched, she studied their moves until she could say to herself, "Wilma, tomorrow . . . tomorrow you're going to see what it feels like to play a little basketball."

Wilma played on the school's team and became a star, setting a new record for high school girls' basketball when she scored 803 points her sophomore year. Wilma also began to run track. At first she wasn't serious about running. She joined the team because she wanted to keep busy after school, and she ran for the sheer pleasure of it. "Running was pure enjoyment for me. I loved the feeling of freedom in running," she once said.

Even though Wilma lost many of her first races, people could see that she was a promising runner. Coach Ed Temple from nearby Tennessee State University was one early fan of Wilma's. He watched her play basketball in high school and run her first races. From the start, he knew she could be a major talent in track and field. Coach Temple asked Wilma's parents to let her go to a summer track camp at Tennessee State. At camp, Wilma ran twenty miles a day. She learned how to run longer, breathe right, and get off to the best possible start.

Losing her first serious races taught Wilma that she could not "always win on natural ability alone, and that there was more to track than just running fast." After her first crushing defeats, Wilma worked harder than ever. "I ran and ran every day, and I acquired this sense of determination, this sense of spirit that I would never, never give up, no matter what else happened."

At the end of the summer of 1956, Wilma competed in an Amateur Athletic Union (AAU) national meet in Philadelphia. She won both the 75-yard and 100-yard dashes. She also ran the anchor leg, or the final section, of a relay race. Her team won. After the meet, Coach Temple said, "Wilma, I think you have a chance to run in the Olympics, and I think you should give it a try."

GOING TO THE OLYMPICS

Two weeks later, Wilma went to Seattle, Washington, for the Olympic tryouts. She was just sixteen years old, but she made the team. Since the Rudolphs were poor, some Clarksville supporters raised money to help Wilma. They bought her new clothes and luggage to take with her to the 1956 Olympics in Melbourne, Australia.

At the Olympics, Wilma failed to advance to the finals in the 200-meter dash. But she ran well in the 400-meter relay. When the American team came in third, Rudolph won her first Olympic medal, a bronze. Winning at the Olympics whetted her appetite for medals. After her experience at Melbourne, Wilma vowed to return in four years and "win more medals, gold ones."

Wilma Rudolph (second from right) and the "Tennessee Tiger Belles" who captured three gold medals at the 1960 Olympic Games.

Wilma Rudolph (second from left) at the 1960 Olympics.

Wilma was already one of the fastest women in the world. During the next four years, she would only get stronger. She entered Tennessee State University and starred on the women's track team. At Tennessee State, Wilma ran track for her longtime friend and supporter, Coach Ed Temple. The coach was famous for his dedication to the track team. He even drove the team to track meets in his car.

Coach Temple made sure his athletes were disciplined and selfless teammates. He had a rule that his runners would run an extra lap for every minute they were late for practice. When Wilma, one of his stars, overslept and showed up 30 minutes late, he stuck to his rule. Wilma ran all 30 extra laps —and made sure she was early for practice the following day.

Training at the highest level, Wilma was determined to be ready for the next Olympics. At the same time, she studied elementary education and psychology. Though a fast runner, she was often known to be late to class!

WINNING GOLD!

1960 was a lucky year for Wilma. But something happened that almost ended Wilma's Olympics before her first race. During practice, she stepped in a hole and turned her ankle. The ankle swelled and stayed sore for the rest of the Rome Olympics. Despite her injury, Wilma advanced to the finals in the 100-meter and 200-meter dashes.

Wilma faced tough odds in the finals. The temperature soared to 100°F. Also, she was running against the world's fastest women. But Wilma ran the 100-meter dash in 11 seconds flat, one of the fastest times ever recorded by a woman runner. The gold medal was hers!

Wilma Rudolph gets the gold in the women's 100 meters in 1960.

The next day, Wilma ran the 200-meter race in the rain. Again, she won. Wilma said to herself, "That's two gold medals down and one to go."

Her last Olympic race was her favorite event. It was the 400-meter relay, and Wilma ran the anchor leg. That meant that her three teammates ran their 100-yard sections of the race first, each one handing a baton to the following runner. Then Wilma ran the last section. She always loved the teamwork of the relay events.

Rudolph runs the anchor leg of the 4x100-meter relay.

Yet it was the teamwork that nearly ended her team's hope for a medal. When Wilma's teammate passed her the baton after the third leg of the race, Wilma fumbled it. Two runners passed her. Now she faced the added pressure of making up her lost time. Still, she surged ahead to win, barely crossing the finish line three-tenths of a second before the second-place runner. Wilma had her third gold medal. She was the first American woman to win three golds.

LIFE AS A CHAMPION

The young American runner became famous. During her stay in Rome, she met the pope. Eager reporters hounded her. Excited fans mobbed her. She was even tagged with a nickname that stuck—"The Tennessee Tornado." Wilma went on to compete in events all over Europe, and continued to win every one.

When she returned to the States, Wilma's hometown held a parade and banquet for her. The parade was the first racially integrated event in the history of Clarksville, Tennessee. Never before had its black and white citizens celebrated together. But Wilma's hometown was not the only community that was proud of her. The whole country celebrated her success.

Rudolph displays her second gold medal for the 200-meter dash at the 1960 Olympics.

Wilma Rudolph meets President John F. Kennedy at the White House on April 14, 1961.

Honors and awards poured in. Wilma traveled to different American cities. She went to formal dinners and gave speeches. She appeared on television. She was even invited to the White House, where she met President John F. Kennedy. In 1961, the Associated Press named Wilma "Female Athlete of the Year."

Wilma was invited to compete in important races that were usually open to male runners only, like the New York Athletic Club Meet and the Penn Relays. "Up to that time, no women had ever run in those meets. I was the first, and the doors have been open ever since to women. I'm proud of that to this day," she recalled. For the first time, women's track was taken as seriously as men's track.

AFTER THE GAMES

The glow of the 1960 Olympics stayed with Wilma Rudolph for the rest of her life. She loved to help young athletes and always had time to help the Olympic movement. She served as a girls' track coach, taught second grade, and worked with community athletic programs.

Wilma never forgot her triumph at Rome. Nor did her many fans. Runners like Florence Griffith Joyner cited Wilma as a great influence. Years after she had hung up her track cleats, President Bill Clinton honored Wilma for her contributions to the sport.

Florence Griffith Joyner, left, embraces Wilma Rudolph. Joyner, who won the 100-meter event at the 1988 Olympics in Seoul, Korea, says Rudolph was a great influence and inspiration.

Her hometown of Clarksville, Tennessee also recognized her achievements. In 1996, Clarksville unveiled a bronze statue of the great runner. Sadly, Wilma Rudolph did not live to see that day. She died of cancer in November of 1994 at the age of fifty-five.

But Wilma Rudolph will always be remembered as the woman who brought worldwide attention to her sport. She is a role model for all of us who have doubted ourselves or had to overcome an illness or racial barrier. Wilma Rudolph, the Tennessee Tornado, achieved her dreams through determination and ceaseless confidence, becoming one of the greatest female runners of all time.

Think About the Selection

1 What challenges did Wilma Rudolph face as a child?

2 Why do you think Wilma was able to overcome polio?

3 Wilma lost many of her earliest races. Describe how she handled these defeats.

4 What can you infer about the way the 1960 Olympics affected the rest of Wilma's life?

Making Connections Wilma Rudolph excelled in her chosen sport. Name a person who excels in another field. Explain why you chose this person.

5.2.1

ISBN 0-618-29494-5

9 780618 294947

90000>

1-51793

HOUGHTON MIFFLIN